*Gulliver Books* is a trademark of Harcourt, Inc., registered in the United States of America and/or other jurisdictions. Library of Congress Cataloging-in-Publication Data: Radunsky, Vladimir. I love you Dude/Vladimir Radunsky. p. cm. Summary: Dude the elephant, having started life as an unwanted doodle on a wall, sets out to try to find his place in the world. [1. Self-realization—Fiction. 2. Graffiti—Fiction. 3. Elephants—Fiction.] I. Title. PZ7.R1226Ial 2005 [Fic]—dc22 2004018485 ISBN 0-15-205176-7
First edition

H G F E D C B A

Printed in Singapore

The display lettering was created by Vladimir Radunsky. Prepress by B-Side Studio Grafico, Roma.
The text type was set in Bodoni.
Color separations by Bright Arts Ltd., Hong Kong
Printed and bound by Tien Wah Press, Singapore
This book was printed on totally chlorine-free Stora Enso Matte paper.
Production supervision by Pascha Gerlinger
Designed by Vladimir Radunsky

# Gulliver Books / Harcourt, Inc.

Orlando   Austin   New York   San Diego   Toronto   London

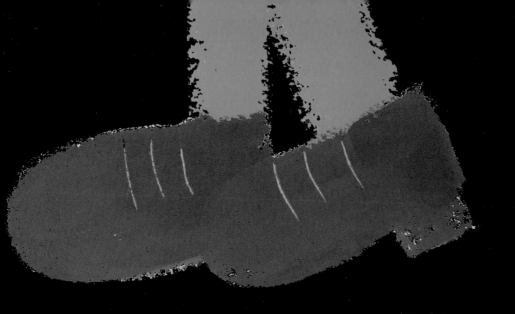

# I Love You Dude

## by V. Radunsky

*translated from the unknown language by E. Radunsky*

7

## *From the Author*

This is a story of a brave young doodle named Dude who makes his way
in the world.

Through dangers and hardships, our hero walks with his trunk held high.
May his true heart serve as a beacon to light our way.

# Chapter 1: The Wall

In the beginning there was only a dirty wall with peeling paint. Some may
remember that on it was a doodle: a girl with huge eyes and a tiny, tiny mouth.
A caption underneath read: LUCY IS A... The rest had been scratched out. Nobody
remembers who made this doodle. But I don't think that it was Lucy herself.

Painters came and quickly and neatly covered the wall in beautiful white paint. How crisp and new it became! Everyone was pleased. Some people even stopped and gaped at this huge, new, clean white wall as if there were something terribly interesting on it. That's how beautiful it was! Well, it was there on that very wall that I was born.

One day a little girl came along (unfortunately I don't even know her name), and on this wall she drew me. I turned out to be an elephant. Now everybody knows that elephants are plump, but she made me skinny. Worse than that, she drew shoes on my feet. Four of them! They made me look really silly. To top it off, she wrote, "I love you Dude." She must have meant me, because Dude is my name. I understood that right away. Dude.

# I Love You Dude

Everyone who passed had a comment. "Tsk, tsk," one woman said. "The wall just got painted and already someone's drawn garbage on it. People have no shame. Why don't they draw on the walls in their houses? I am going to the police right away to complain."

What a way to start a life—sitting here on this wall, and everybody staring at me. Nobody was happy with me. There were no presents for baby Dude. No grandmothers or grandfathers came to pinch my cheeks. No one to say, "Kootchy-koo, kootchy-koo." Of course, above me it said, "I love you Dude," but the writing was so sloppy and crooked that no one even paid attention to it.

And now the police? I was alone, ashamed, and miserable.

I decided to run away from the wall. As far away as possible. As far as my feet in these stupid shoes would carry me. Good-bye, wall!

# Chapter 2: To Get Away!

To get away! But where to? What would I do when I got there? And where would I live? And what would I eat? But what does food matter when you're a doodle, a doodle named Dude.

# Chapter 3: Shopping Around

I walked for a long time along endless streets. Endless shop windows with their endless lights were blinking before my eyes. People hurried about, minding their own business, and nobody cared about me. What a crowd of people! What a crowd of things!

Then in the thick of this terrible crowd, I saw them: cups! Right in a shop window. So many! Each with its own beautiful message. And every single one of them was about love. There were ones that I especially liked: "I love Mom" and "I love Dad." How lovely it would be to have and to love your mom and dad. But my favorite was a yellow cup, not because it was yellow (I may like blue or green better), but because there was nothing written on it.

No one was watching, so I ran up to the window and…jumped right onto the cup!

It was great! There we all were on one shelf: "I love NY," "I love NYPD," "I love Lucy," and "I love you Dude" (that's me). What a nice bunch! Honestly, that cup and I were a perfect fit!

After all, am I any worse than NYPD? Why shouldn't I be loved the same as him (or her)?

People passed by our window. Some stopped and looked at the cups and at me, Dude.

One man walked in and bought "I love Lucy." Good-bye, "I love Lucy." I did not even find out who you were. Well, I hope you are happy in your new home.

Suddenly I felt somebody lift me off the shelf. I didn't even have time to see who it was before I was wrapped in paper. In an instant I found myself in total darkness. They bought me! They bought me! I was in a bag. I was being carried somewhere. But where? And by whom?

The next thing I remember was a bright light and a sweet voice, a girl's voice: "Oh, Dude! What a cute Dude! Thank you, Daddy. Please, please may I have my milk with Dude?"

And a wonderful, peaceful life began for me.

Each morning the little girl appeared at breakfast like a princess with her court: all her dolls and one very friendly teddy bear. He looked at me so kindly that I thought, *I have found a friend.* There was also a huge stuffed elephant who looked a little bit like me, but pink and soft.

Each morning the little girl drank milk from my cup. Sometimes we even talked. At least she talked constantly—"I love you, Dude. I love you, Dude"—and laughed.

This is the kind of life I had always dreamed of: a life of love and respect.

# Chapter 4: The Mean Aunt

But it was not to be. My cruel fate had decided otherwise. Even now I cannot tell this story without a shudder.

One day my little girl's aunt came to visit. I did not trust that aunt from the very first. "Just look at that miserable thing!" she said. "What a creature! Where did it come from?" Suddenly I was in her terrible clutches. "How about a cup of coffee? A nice hot cup of coffee will do me good right now. Pour some right into this cup. Dude and I will have a little coffee together. Ha-ha-ha!"

What a nasty woman. "Dude and I..."—as if I could drink coffee!

After that, everything became kind of foggy. That coffee was boiling! Why, it was hot enough to fry eggs on my trunk!

I leaped from the the cup and, frankly, I don't even know how I managed to scramble outside. But I know this: I did not stop running.

# Chapter 5: It's a Jungle Out There . . .

I ran like a wounded tiger (no, like a wounded elephant). I was blinded by headlights and deafened by blaring horns. Suddenly brakes screeched and two giant truck eyes bulged in front of my face. Terrified, I jumped away and scurried up the nearest pole.

I must have climbed quite high. I could still hear the sounds of the cars below, but now they were muffled. It was spacious and quiet here. I wasn't in anybody's way. I could rest for a while and think.

It was getting dark. Peering down I saw lights coming up here and there all around me.

Somewhere out there, there were people and children and their cats and dogs and their birds and pet hamsters—all loving and respecting one another and making one another happy. But I...I did not live anywhere. Nobody loved me or missed me. No one even knew I existed.

I thought about the cup and the little girl. Perhaps she was sitting with her mother and father and watching television. Some funny cartoons or a nice movie. She might be looking for me. It could be that she wanted some milk.

*Oh, I would give anything to be sitting in that warm kitchen right now, drinking milk with her. If it weren't for that monstrous woman and her awful coffee...*
The thought of it made me so sad I started to cry.

I was startled from my sad thoughts by voices down below shouting, "Way to go, Dude!" "Look at the Dude on top!" And then I heard a child's voice: "Run, Dude, run! They're coming to get you!"

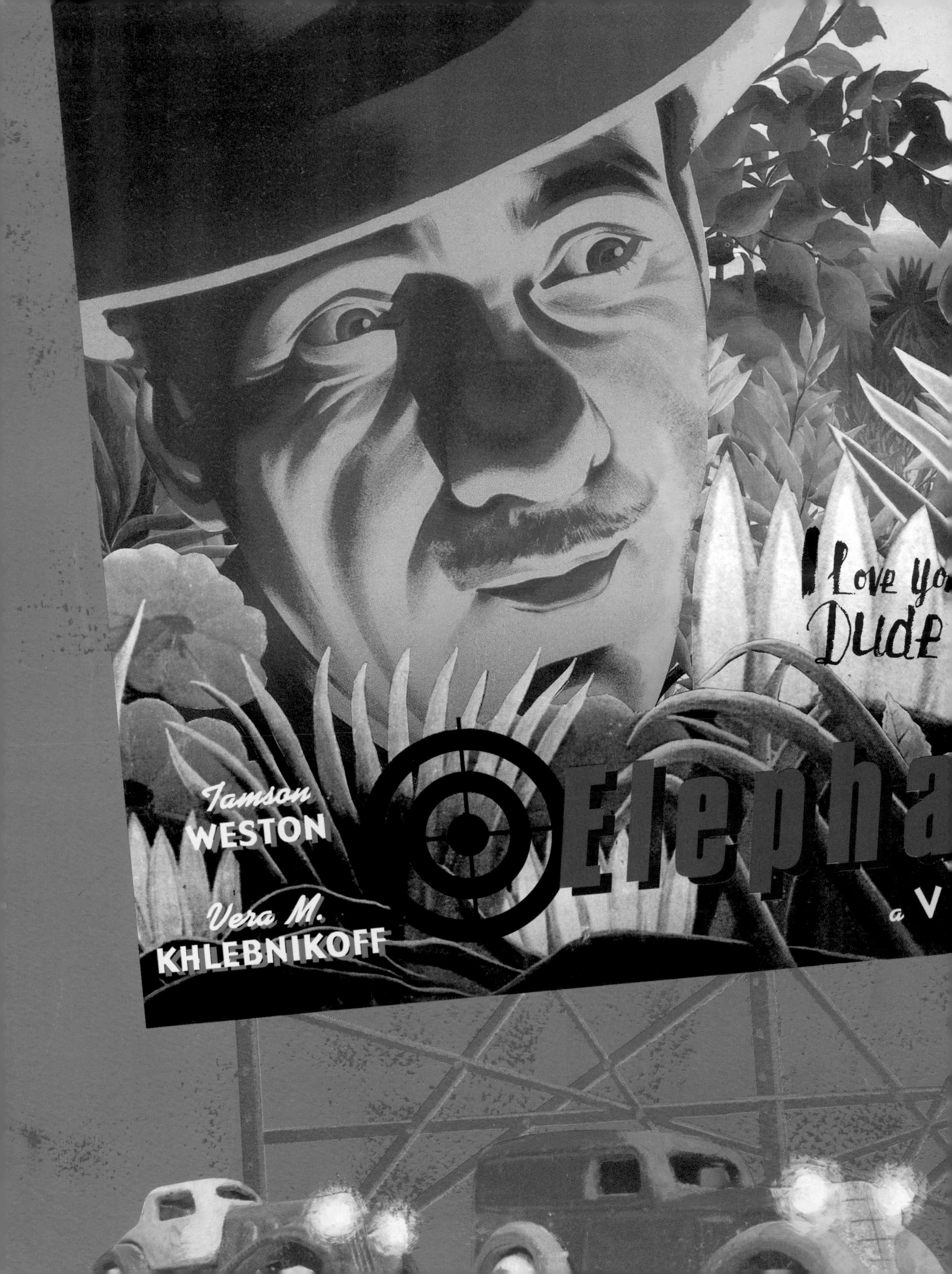

# Chapter 6: Du

I ran and ran and ran and ran and ran.
And ran and ran and ran and ran and ran and ran.

# de's On the Run

And ran and ran and ra
and ran and ran and ra
and ran.

# Chapter 7: Tremendous Belly

Before I knew it, I was at the edge of the sea. The sun was setting, and there wasn't a soul in sight. But what did I want with the rest of the world? Nobody cared about me, anyway.

The beach was empty, but here and there lay cast-off things, forgotten like me.

In the sand somebody drew a pretty house with a person next to it. He even had a name: Arnold. *And why not me, I thought, Dude? I could lie right here in the sand and the sun, too. I could be a tanned Dude! People would admire me!*

I lay right down. Ah, what bliss! The sky was blue, a seagull flew by...(I wonder, can seagulls read? Probably not. But perhaps they could read something as simple as "I love you Dude.")

I felt completely happy and fell asleep, lulled by the sound of the waves....

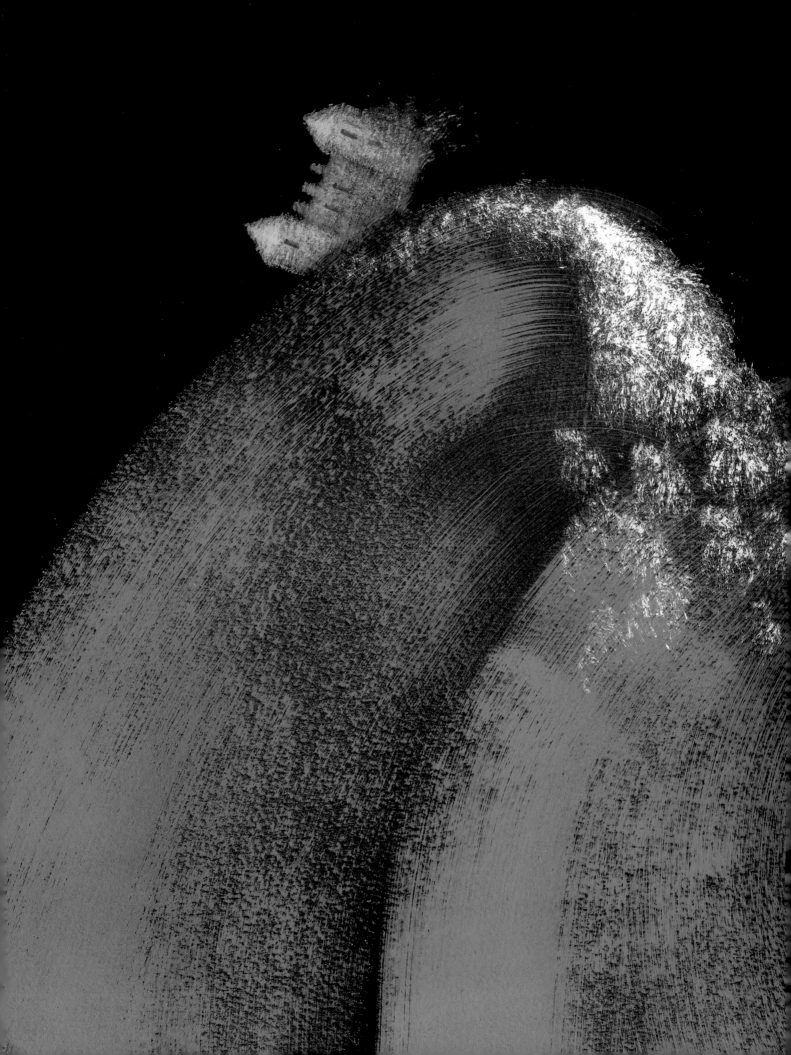

ARNOLD

Waves! Oh my god! The waves were rolling in. In my sleep I did not realize that they were sneaking up closer and closer. One wave just licked the sand castle, and then another, her twin sister, gobbled it up. And then came Arnold's turn. The next wave grabbed poor Arnold and swept away his name. Surely I was next!

I jumped up in terror and galloped away as fast as I could. Away...into the darkness.

That night I imagined waves rushing at me. But little by little, the surf subsided and I fell asleep again.

When I awoke, it was a glorious morning. The sun was shining. People were lazily filling up the beach. Somewhere a child's voice called, "Mama, Mama, where is Arnold? Where did he go?" I didn't want to upset the little girl, so I kept quiet. Let her think that Arnold just went for a walk.

People kept coming and coming. And how different they all were! Short and tall, fat and skinny, hairy and hairless, tanned and very pale. Some even had tattoos.

Right in front of me a man with a tremendous belly plopped down. This one had the most amazing tattoos. Pretty pictures everywhere, but nothing on his belly! Could I be another tattoo? It might be pleasant, living on this soft, tremendous belly; sleeping on it, rising and falling, rising and falling, as though in a cradle. Nice and cozy.

In winter, he could put on a sweater and a jacket—I'd be warm. Summers we'd spend at the beach. We could even swim. (I wonder if he can swim.)

But as soon as I imagined it, I realized it was not the life for me—always hiding under shirts, rarely seeing human faces...no. My heart longed for greater things.

And then I clearly understood. The important thing is to have a purpose in life and not quit until you find it. I had been lucky once.

I knew I would be lucky again!

# Chapter 8: Seven from Paris

Feeling light as a feather, I skipped along the beach.

Suddenly a curious thing caught my eye. It was something I had never seen before: an odd house made of striped fabric. All around it were flags flying in the wind. On the side in great big red letters was written CIRCUS and below that there were seven elephants! One big family. And they were all smiling.

Just then two policemen walked by, talking. They stopped and stared at the picture. I thought they were going to grab the elephants and arrest them.

But instead one of them said, "Wow! Pretty big, these elephants. Much bigger than a horse." And the other said, "Yup, you gotta have a long ladder to get up on one of these."

Only then did I notice what was written underneath:

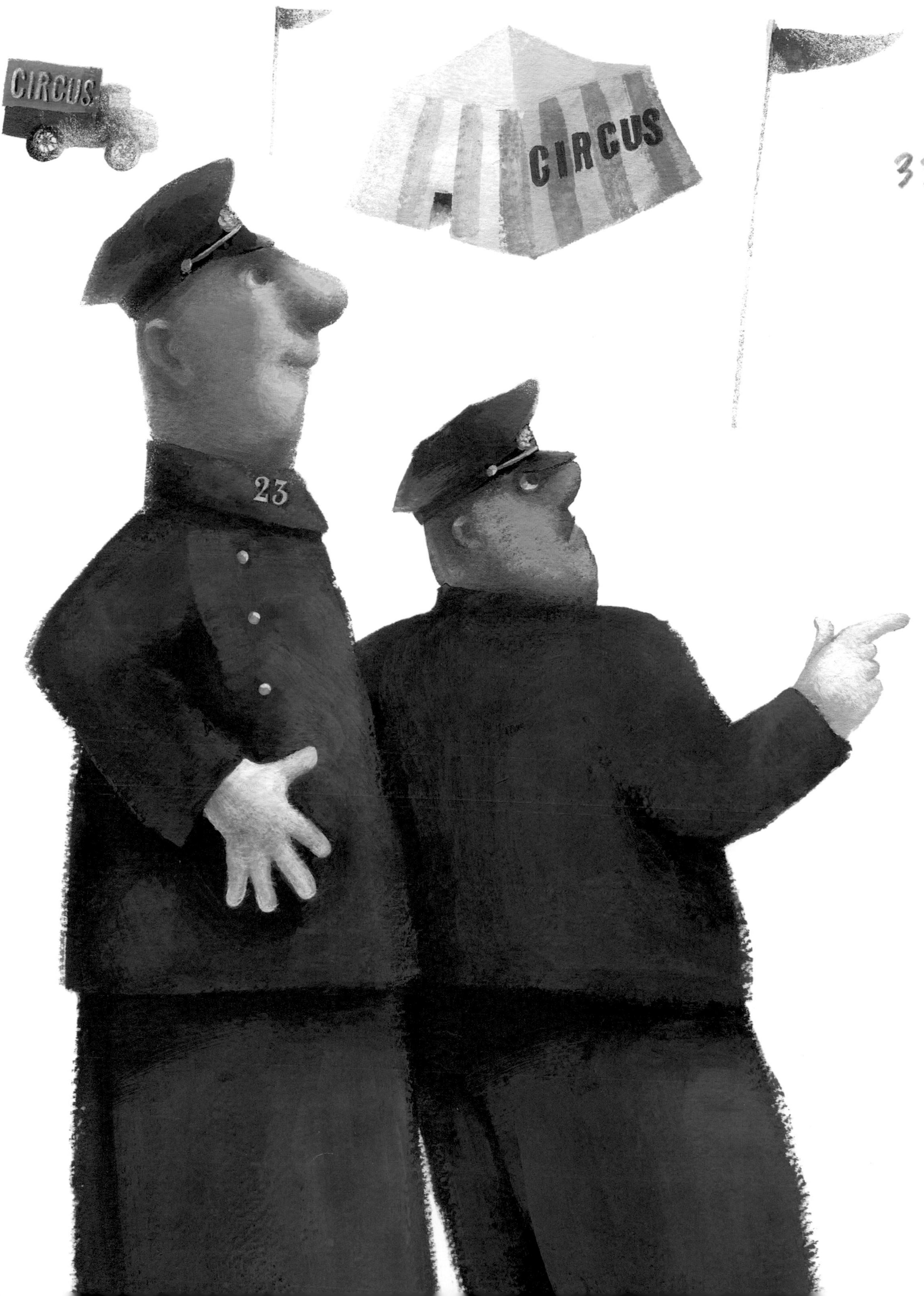
CIRCUS
CIRCUS
23

RCUS

GRACEFUL AND INTRICATE

I was so curious that I decided to sneak inside, meet these elephants, and discover their secret.

I crept quietly inside the circus tent, which was what they called this beautiful striped house. Adults and children were streaming in from all directions.

Inside there was a giant ring, and in the ring a giant bald man with a huge mustache was dressed in shiny black boots and a red and gold jacket. He raised his arms, cracked his whip, and shouted, "Mesdames and messieurs!" (Was that French? I didn't know.)

And then I saw them! All seven of them. They were enormous—even the smallest of them! And so handsome! The orchestra began to play and the elephants started to dance.

All of a sudden, the lights came down. The mother elephant climbed onto the father elephant, and all the children climbed on one another. They made a pyramid all the way up to the peak of the tent. You could hardly see the top!

The audience held its breath. In the silence an old man sneezed violently, making the pyramid sway. But nobody noticed because right at that moment

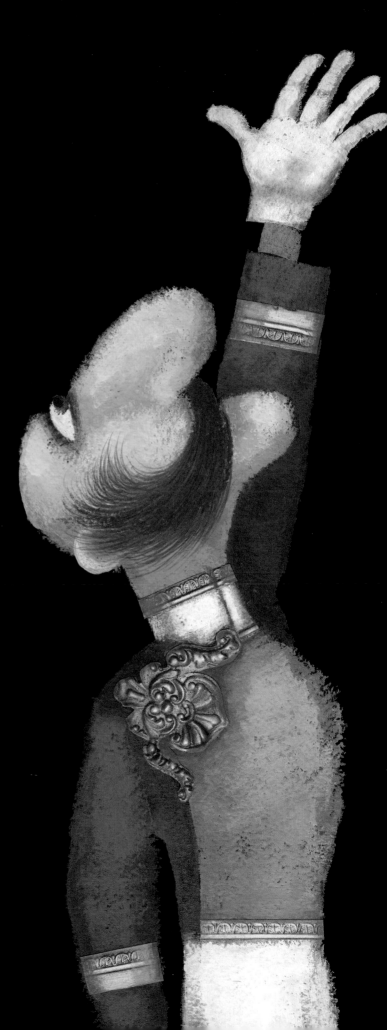

there was a drumroll, the lights sparkled, and the elephants trumpeted all at once. Applause erupted like thunder.

I thought my heart would leap from my chest, so fiercely did it pound. Then I was struck by a thought: *This must be my place. This is my mission in life. I must be here in the circus, performing with the elephants! They will embrace me as their own. My home will be the world: from Paris, France, to Paris, Texas. Everywhere I go audiences will applaud and people will admire me.*

The show was over; the happy crowd was leaving the circus. One chubby little boy climbed on top of his father and yelled, "I am an elephant! I am an elephant!"

I quickly ran outside. The boy's words echoed in my ears. *I am an elephant, I am an elephant! YES! I am an elephant! Me, Dude! I–AM–AN–elephant!*

Wasting no time, I jumped up and fell in behind the smallest elephant. But no sooner had I made myself comfortable, than that bald-headed man with the mustache came out. He saw me right away.

"What on earth is that?" he asked. "Are you some kind of clown? Look how skinny you are! You call yourself an elephant? And what's with the shoes? No way, Dude. You can't be for real. You look like…a doodle. Ha-ha! Get it? DOODle. Du-u-u-de…no way." He laughed nastily and pulled me off the wall.

Oh, what shame. My hopes were crushed. No family, no applause, no Paris. I wished I'd never been drawn. What was there to live for?

# BREATHTAKING S

## IN PINK UNDERWEAR. NOW SE

# Chapter 9: The Ultimate Dude

I walked all day, not knowing where. I couldn't even think. I was all alone in the world.

Exhausted, I fell to the sidewalk. People walked over me without even noticing. A child rolled over me on his scooter. I didn't feel a thing; I didn't care. Somebody spit out a piece of gum; it landed right on me. Before, I would have been angry, but now it simply didn't matter. Soon I would not exist. Little by little I would be wiped out. Erased from the world. Perhaps it was for the best.

I'm just dirt! A doodle! I'm no good!

What happened next seems like a dream. I heard somebody calling me: "Dude, Dude! I love you, Dude!"

A heavenly voice was saying, "What deep words. How they speak to me. I love you, Dude! What a beautiful drawing. How expressive! It doesn't belong here on this dirty sidewalk. It should be where everyone can appreciate it!"

I was lovingly cleaned, scraped free of chewing gum, and dressed in an ornate gold frame. I was carefully taken to a museum and hung on a wall for all to see.

"Dude, this is your home now and these are your neighbors. This is a Picasso and this is a Matisse. I'm sure you will like one another."

Just then a whole crowd of people rushed in. "Genius! Extraordinary!" "Just look at this Dude. What a face!" "How simple and dignified! Subtle, yet provocative!" "Oh, and the shoes! How clever. How elegant!"

Every day, tour group after tour group came to see me and my new friends. Children of all ages, adults, students, senior citizens—they all admired us.

Never had I known such happiness, not even when I was on a cup filled with milk. At last I could bring joy to people. I wished those Seven From Paris could see me now. Too bad they do not allow elephants in the museum.

# Chapter 10: Working Hours

Do not imagine for a moment that this was an easy life, though. Oh no.
Picasso, Matisse, and I all worked very hard:

Tuesday–Friday
10:00 A.M.–5:00 P.M.

\*

Saturday, Sunday
10:00 A.M.–7:00 P.M.

\*

# Monday
# Closed

On Mondays it was quiet: It was cleaning day. Someone dusted me with a special duster. I hung quietly and remembered my previous life. It seemed as though several lifetimes had passed: the girl with the cup and her mean aunt, the hunters, the scary waves, the Belly, Mr. Baldhead with Mustache, Seven From Paris, and the wonderful woman who saved me.

the ENd OF MY STORY.